Little Red Riding Hood

First published in 2008 by
Franklin Watts
338 Euston Road
London
NW1 3BH

Franklin Watts Australia
Level 17/207 Kent Street
Sydney
NSW 2000

A CIP catalogue record for this book is available
from the British Library.

ISBN 978 0 7496 7901 9 (hbk)
ISBN 978 0 7496 7907 1 (pbk)

Series Editor: Melanie Palmer
Series Advisor: Dr Barrie Wade
Series Designer: Peter Scoulding

Printed in China

Franklin Watts is a division of
Hachette Children's Books,
an Hachette Livre UK company.

Little Red Riding Hood

by Anne Walter and Marjorie Dumortier

W

FRANKLIN WATTS

LONDON•SYDNEY

Long ago, a girl called
Little Red Riding Hood
lived in a village by a wood.

5

One day, her mother said, "Little Red Riding Hood, your granny is poorly. Please take her this basket to cheer her up."

"But remember – don't talk to any strangers on the way," she added.

Little Red Riding Hood set off
straight away. She had not gone far
when she felt a tap on her shoulder.

8

It was the big bad wolf!
"What a tasty snack she will
make," he thought.

9

"Are you lost, little girl?"
asked the wolf, smiling.
"No," said Little Red Riding Hood.
"I'm going to visit my granny.
She lives by the stream."

"Really!" grinned the wolf,
licking his lips.

11

Litte Red Riding Hood picked up
the basket and hurried on her way.

The wolf also rushed to Granny's
house. "Granny lunch with little
girl pudding – delicious!" he thought.

The wolf knocked on Granny's door.

"Come in, dear," called Granny.

The wolf let himself in and
swallowed Granny whole!

Then the wolf quickly put on
a nightgown and frilly cap,
and got into granny's bed.

16

Soon, Little Red Riding Hood arrived.

"Granny, it's Little Red Riding Hood."

"Come in dear!" called the wolf in
his squeakiest voice.

When Little Red Riding Hood
went inside, she could hardly
recognise Granny.

"Oh Granny, you sound terrible!"
said Little Red Riding Hood.
"I have a cold, dear," said the wolf.

"Granny, what big ears you have!"
said Little Red Riding Hood.

"All the better to hear you with,"
replied the wolf.

"Granny, what big eyes you have!"
said Little Red Riding Hood.
"All the better to see you with,"
replied the wolf.

23

"Granny, what big teeth you have!"
said Little Red Riding Hood.

24

"All the better to EAT you with!"
roared the wolf and he leapt out
of the bed.

25

Little Red Riding Hood ran as fast as she could out of Granny's house. "Help! Help!" she screamed.

The wolf tried to run after her,
but he tripped over the nightgown.

Luckily, a woodcutter was nearby.
He grabbed the wolf and made
him cough up Granny.

Then the woodcutter chased the
wolf far away, deep into the wood.

Little Red Riding Hood and Granny
sat down to share the tasty cake
from Mother's basket.

"I promise never talk to strangers again," said Little Red Riding Hood.

Hopscotch has been specially designed to fit the requirements of the Literacy Framework. It offers real books by top authors and illustrators for children developing their reading skills. There are 55 Hopscotch stories to choose from:

* **hardback**